OCTONAUTS

and the Flying Fish

The daring crew of the Octopod are ready to embark on an exciting new mission!

INKLING OCTOPUS
(Professor)

KWAZII CAT
(Lieutenant)

PESO PENGUIN
(Medic)

BARNACLES BEAR
(Captain)

TWEAK BUNNY
(Engineer)

SHELLINGTON SEA OTTER
(Field Researcher)

DASHI DOG
(Photographer)

TUNIP THE VEGIMAL
(Ship's Cook)

EXPLORE . RESCUE . PROTECT

OCTONAUTS™

and the Flying Fish

SIMON AND SCHUSTER

Professor Inkling was reading a very special book to the Octonauts.

"My great-grandfather wrote all about his travels," explained the Professor. "There's a mystery in here that's never been solved."

Kwazii clapped his hands. He loved a mystery!

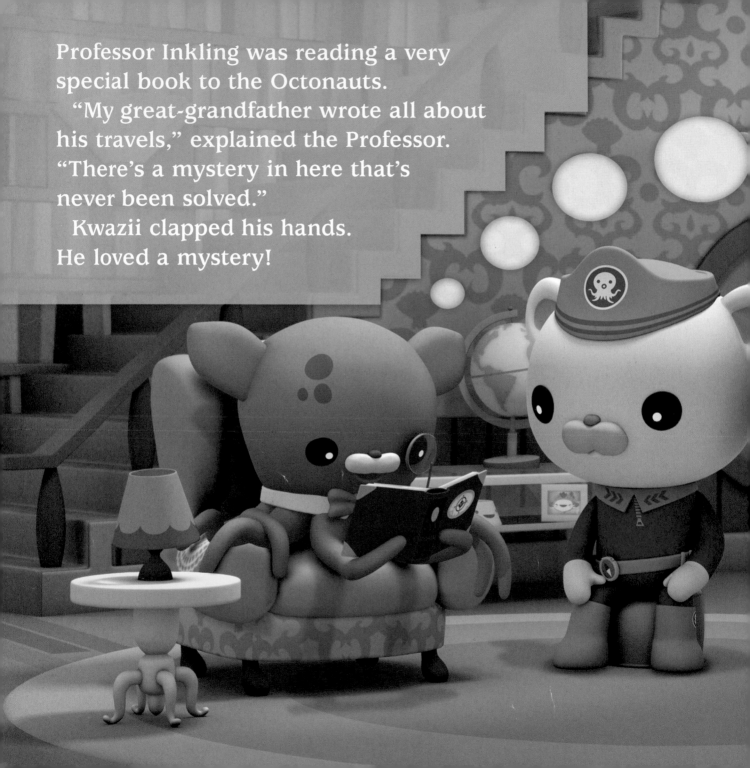

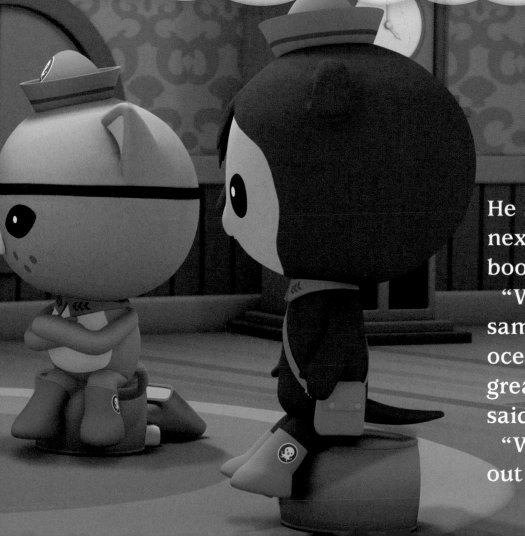

Professor Inkling began.

"It was a beautiful, starry night. The water was calm and smooth when all of a sudden I saw something leap out of the water, something remarkable, and that something was a..."

He stopped. The next page of the book was missing! "We're in the same part of the ocean as your great-grandfather," said Barnacles. "We must find out what he saw!"

The Octonauts rushed to the launch bay.

"Open the Octohatch, Tweak!" called the Captain, leaping into the GUP-A.

Kwazii watched Shellington put the Professor's book into his waterproof satchel. They had to make sure it didn't get wet – the precious journal had never been taken out of the library.

When they got to the surface, the ocean was quiet and still. Kwazii decided to check the map at the back of the Professor's book.

"Why don't I hold it for you?" suggested Shellington.

"I can hold it meself!" insisted Kwazii.

"Look at that!" gasped Barnacles. A silvery school of flying fish was soaring over their heads!

Kwazii and Shellington both tugged at the satchel. Suddenly the bag was sent spinning into the air! The pair gasped as a passing flying fish caught the strap on its tail fin.

"Yeeeooowww!"

wailed Kwazii.

He made a brave lunge for the bag, but missed, landing in the water with a p-l-o-p! "We have got to get the Professor's book back," cried the Captain.

🐙 FACT: **SPEEDY ESCAPE**

When flying fish want to make a quick getaway, they leap out of the water.

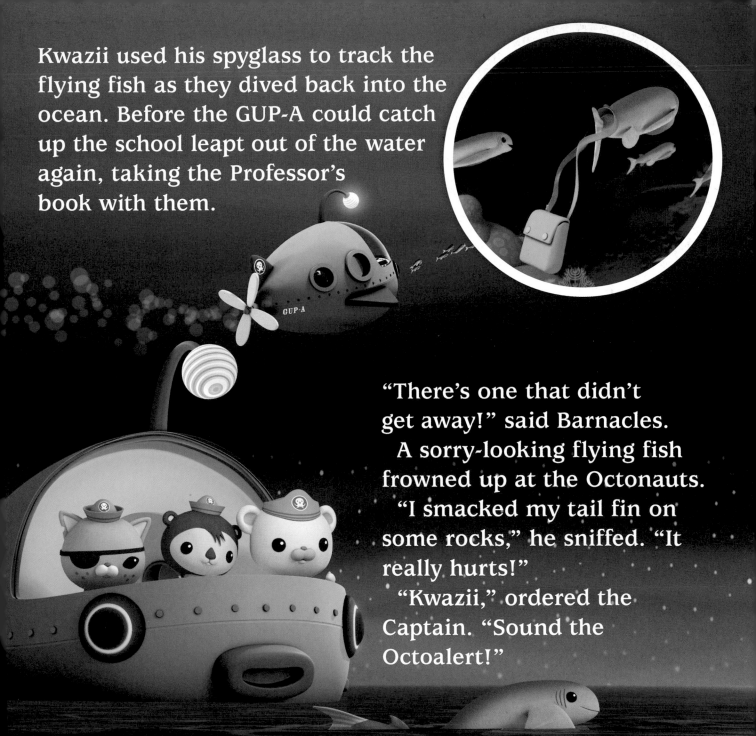

Kwazii used his spyglass to track the flying fish as they dived back into the ocean. Before the GUP-A could catch up the school leapt out of the water again, taking the Professor's book with them.

"There's one that didn't get away!" said Barnacles.

A sorry-looking flying fish frowned up at the Octonauts. "I smacked my tail fin on some rocks," he sniffed. "It really hurts!"

"Kwazii," ordered the Captain. "Sound the Octoalert!"

"Octonauts, to

the launch **bay!**"

When the GUP-A docked, Peso
was ready and waiting.
   "What seems to be the trouble?"
he asked, jumping into
the water.
   The flying fish lifted
up his hurt tail fin.
   Peso pulled out a
bandage. With a bit
of rest, the fish
would be flying
again in no
time!

The Professor was delighted to meet Peso's new patient. "You must be the remarkable thing that my great-grandfather saw," he cried. "I'll add that to my book right away."

Kwazii and Shellington both gulped.

"We… sort of… lost the book," admitted Kwazii. "But we'll get it back for ye – on my honour as an **Octonaut, we will!**"

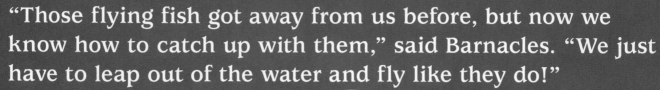

"Those flying fish got away from us before, but now we know how to catch up with them," said Barnacles. "We just have to leap out of the water and fly like they do!"

Tweak reached for her spanner. "I'm on it, 'Cap!" she grinned.

🐙 FACT: **FLYING**

PECTORAL FIN

TAIL FIN

Flying fish use their special pectoral, or side, fins to help them glide.

Tweak got to work on Kwazii's sub. With the flying fish's help, she could make just the right changes to the GUP-B to get it into the air.

"I use my tail fin to push myself out of the water," explained the fish. "Then I spread out my pectoral fins."

"Fascinating!" marvelled Shellington.

The GUP-B was ship-shape and ready to fly before you could say 'buncha munchy crunchy carrots'!
   "I've added pectoral fins and a fully-adjustable tail fin," said Tweak.

Before the mission could begin, Peso gave his patient one final check-up.

"My tail fin doesn't hurt at all now," said the flying fish.

"He's ready to fly, Captain!" nodded the proud medic.

Captain Barnacles ordered everyone into the gups.

"With your help," he nodded, "we'll find your friends and get the Professor's book back. Octonauts, let's do this!"

The little flying fish darted through the ocean, followed by Kwazii in the GUP-B. Barnacles, Peso and Shellington whooshed behind in the GUP-A.

Up ahead, the fish's friends shimmered in the water.

"There they are, mateys!" cried Kwazii, "and there's the Professor's book!"

It was time to put the GUP-B to the test.

Kwazii zoomed up to the surface at top speed. Suddenly he was flying through the air, just like the runaway fish!

"Look at them go!" gasped Peso.

Kwazii soared through the moonlit sky. He jumped out of the cockpit, then made a grab for the fish with the satchel on its tail.

"I've got it!" he shouted, waving the bag in the air. "Thank you, flying fishy!"

Professor Inkling was thrilled to have his precious book back again.

"Octonauts," he announced. "Thanks to you, we can now add the ending to my great-grandfather's adventure!"

"Aye!" cried Kwazii.

The Professor opened the book and began to read once again.

"It was a beautiful, starry night. The water was calm and smooth when all of a sudden I saw something leap out of the water, something remarkable, and that something was a... magnificent school of flying fish!"

It was the perfect end to a perfect Octonauts adventure!

Calling all Octonauts! When Professor Inkling told us about his great-grandfather's mystery, we had to find out more! The silvery flying fish uses its special fins to soar high above the ocean waves.

FACT FILE: THE FLYING FISH

The flying fish is an expert at speedy escapes. It swims fast to the surface before taking to the air!

≋ It lives in open water.

✳ It eats tiny floating plants and animals.

OCTOFACTS:

1. The flying fish uses its tail fins to push itself up and out of the water.

2. Flying helps it to get away from bigger fish, such as tuna and marlin.

3. When the flying fish takes to the skies, it can glide for up to 400 metres!

OCTONAUTS

Dive into action with these super, splashtastic Octonauts books!

and the Decorator Crab

and the Flying Fish

and the Orcas

and the Giant Squid

and the Monster Map
A Lift-the-Flap Adventure!

and the Whale Shark

and the Electric Torpedo Rays

and the Great Penguin Race

Go Go Gups!
GUP-C   GUP-D
GUP-E

Ready for Action in the GUP – A!

Meet the Crew

Discover
Little Library
lore!
Rescue!   Protect!
Save the Day!